First published in Great Britain in 1994
by Simon & Schuster Young Books
Reprinted in 1996 by Macdonald Young Books

Macdonald Young Books
61 Western Road, Hove,
East Sussex BN3 1JD

Reprinted in 1994

Typeset in 15/23pt Meridien by Goodfellow & Egan Ltd, Cambridge, England
Printed and bound in Belgium by Proost International Book Productions

British Library Cataloguing in Publication Data available

ISBN 0 7500 1461 X
ISBN 0 7500 1462 8 (pbk)

Helen Muir

The Twenty Ton Chocolate Mountain

Illustrated by Robert Geary

MACDONALD YOUNG BOOKS

For Clare

Sports Special

The new teacher, Mr McWeedie, had a long nose. He wore rings on his long thin fingers and odd socks on his long spindly legs. His pockets bulged with bits of old rubbish. His shoes were like boats.

He walked very fast with his head in the air and his arms swinging. The rudest children walked behind, copying him.

Mr McWeedie did look a bit nutty. And he was odd.

He didn't teach the children much about reading or adding up. He told them about spaghetti trees and singing sunflowers and the Twenty Ton Chocolate Mountain.

Someone called him Weedy the Weed and then they all did.

He rode his bicycle right through the school doors and into the classroom.

The Head put a notice up by the coat pegs. 'NO CYCLING!'

"Mr McWeedie cycles past my bedroom window every night," said a shy boy called Tom who lived ten floors up in a high block. But nobody believed that.

The children didn't really know what to believe about Mr McWeedie. Out on walks he showed them birds' eggs and fox cubs and fairy rings in the grass. He stood on his head in his tartan trousers and talked to plants. He hid behind trees, hooting like an owl.

"He's probably a wizard," Tom said, but nobody listened.

As Mr McWeedie was a fast walker, he enjoyed walking races.

"First back to school gets a bite at the Twenty Ton Chocolate Mountain!" He blew his whoopee whistle, "Go!"

While the excited children bumped and fell over each other, Weedy pranced past them, swinging his thin arms. Nobody won so much as a Malteser.

The children looked everywhere for the chocolate mountain. Nobody had ever heard of it. "Is it in your garden?" they asked Mr McWeedie.

"Nope."

"Is it in the EEC?"

"Left turn at the singing sunflowers." He drew a map on somebody's T-shirt. "Straight on past the spaghetti trees."

A cheeky girl called Ella put her hand up. "My dad says there aren't any singing flowers or spaghetti trees."

"Oh does he?" Mr McWeedie replied, "And I suppose he doesn't believe in twenty ton chocolate mountains either?"

"No he doesn't."

"Hmmm . . ." Mr McWeedie stared crossly down his long thin nose.

"Mr McWeedie is a fast walker," said the Head. "He can also stand on his head. He will be organising our school sports day."

"My dad always wins the fathers' race," Ella boasted. "He hates chocolate."

"My dad always comes last," Tom said sadly. "He loves chocolate."

Ella poked him with her ruler. "You're always last yourself, mouseface, so you won't get any."

As the school sports drew nearer, Mr McWeedie walked faster still, talking to himself. While they helped him get ready for the great day, the other children forgot about the chocolate mountain. But Tom didn't.

From his bedroom window he saw Weedy cycling away above the trees but he didn't tell anyone. He wished sports day was over. He hated it.

Ella's dad, Mr Spanker-Bacon, arrived first at the sports in his fast car, dressed to win the fathers' race as usual.

"Welcome to our big event!" cried the Head, who liked rich people. "Mr McWeedie's in charge."

"From what I hear he's not fit to be in charge of a dead cat," Mr Spanker-Bacon boomed. "Is he going to talk to the flowers?"

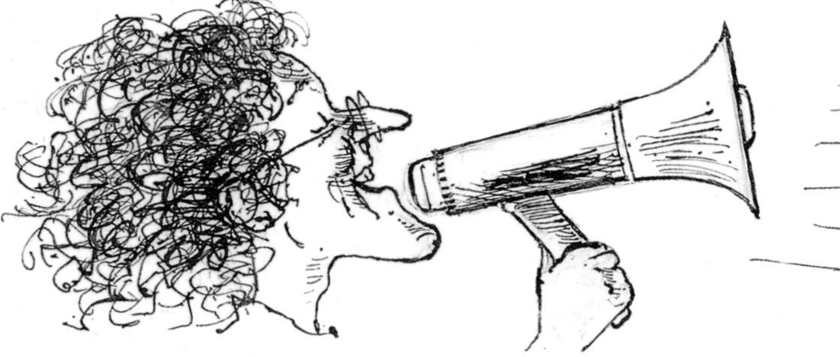

The first race was the egg and spoon. Mr McWeedie darted about with his megaphone calling out names as the children lined up. "Clare, Lani, Marlon, Emily, Jennifer, Sinead, Simeon, Alex, Marit, Maya, Freddie, Lucy, Jay, Samantha, Daniel, Harry, Ella, Tom."

"Mr McWeedie's a thin man for someone who likes a lot of chocolate and spaghetti," said Tom's mother.

"All righty! Eyes on eggs!" Mr McWeedie blew his whistle.

The children ran. Their parents cheered. Ella bumped Tom who dropped his egg.

Simeon won.
Ella came second.
Tom was last.

Tom was last in the shopping race. And the hopping. He felt awful. He wanted to go home.

Seeing Tom's sad face, Mr McWeedie stopped to pat his shoulder. "Come and help me with the sacks for the fathers' race."

"We're waiting, Mr McWeedie!" called Mr Spanker-Bacon, who wasn't used to waiting for anyone. He picked up Mr McWeedie's megaphone and boomed into it. "Okay you dads! Let's show 'em!"

"My dad'll show 'em," Ella giggled. "He always wins."

"My megaphone, Spanker, *thank yer*!" As Mr McWeedie grabbed it, the starting tape tangled round their legs.

They bounced into each other. An alarm clock went off in Mr McWeedie's pocket and Mr Spanker-Bacon's lovely baseball cap flew off into the mud.

"What a nutter!" he gasped angrily, as Mr McWeedie trod on it.

Mr Spanker-Bacon was still scowling as all the fathers climbed into their sacks. But at the whistle he shuffled off into the lead.

"Come on Dad!" the children shouted.

Suddenly there was a big bang! Mr Spanker-Bacon turned three somersaults. Sparks and a strange stink filled the air as he landed on his back punching and kicking. Four other fathers fell on top of him.

Tom laughed but Mr McWeedie was *doubled up*. That's when Tom *knew*. He *was* a wizard!

The last race was the sprint. Tom kept his eyes on Weedy and wished. He knew he was going to win.

He passed Ella then Harry then Alex. He went like the wind. WH..O..O..SH!

When Tom went up for his prize he thought Mr McWeedie winked because he'd guessed the secret of getting to the Twenty Ton Chocolate Mountain.

Ella's Birthday Present

Now that Tom knew Weedy really was a wizard, he dreamt of going to the Twenty Ton Chocolate Mountain all the time.

Twice he'd stared hard at Mr McWeedie, started to wish, then stopped. He was a bit scared of this new power. He made some small wishes while he was getting used to it. He made it rain and he'd hidden forty packets of crisps under his bed.

He tried his powers out on Ella Spanker-Bacon on one of Mr McWeedie's walks.

When Mr McWeedie stopped in a field to talk to some buttercups, Ella Spanker-Bacon copied him behind his back to make the other children laugh.

"Can buttercups sing like the singing sunflowers, Mr McWeedie?" she asked in a silly voice. "We can't hear anything. Ask them to sing Teddy Bears' Picnic."

Tom wanted to tell her to shut up but she went on and on.

"Mr McWeedie, make the buttercups sing louder, oh go on *please*. Tell 'em me and Samantha want to hear Teddy Bears' Picnic. Hey, can I take them singing buttercups home for my birthday party?"

Tom stared at the wizard then shut his eyes and wished. "Please make Ella Spanker-Bacon fall in a cowpat."

When Tom opened his eyes again, Ella was sitting in a cowpat, looking surprised.

Mr McWeedie was laughing.

"Ooh pooh!" Jay shouted. "You're a stinker! Get off!"

Shrieking, the other children held their noses and ran away from her.

Ella had to take her clothes off and walk home in Mr McWeedie's old jacket. She was in a real rage. "I'm not asking any of you pinheads to my party now."

"It won't be a party if nobody comes," Lucy said, "and you won't get any presents."

"I'll get presents, don't you worry," Ella sniffed. "My dad will buy me anything I want. He owns the Bite-up Bacon Company."

"He never," said Marlon. "What's he going to buy you then?"

"Why should I tell you, ratface? It's a secret anyway."

So Ella swanked and showed off while they all tried to find out what she was getting for her birthday.

"I know something she won't be getting," Tom said. "The Twenty Ton Chocolate Mountain."

"That's what I'm getting!" Ella shouted, "Yum yum yum!" And she asked her father that very night.

Mr Spanker-Bacon didn't like chocolate but he did like admiration. With his big bacon business, and a huge heap of chocolate in the garden, he would be the talk of the town. He decided to buy the mountain for Ella's birthday.

He roared round to see Mr McWeedie in his fast car.

Mr McWeedie opened the door in his tartan trousers and cycling helmet. "The Twenty Ton Chocolate Mountain?" He laughed. "It's not for sale."

Mr Spanker-Bacon glared. "Come off it, McWeedie! I'm a rich man. There's always a price. Let's have it."

"No," said Mr McWeedie.

"I told you he wouldn't," Tom said to Ella.

But Mr Spanker-Bacon never took no for an answer. The more noes he got, the angrier he grew.

Two days before Ella's party he bashed on the door and shouted: "If that blooming chocolate is not in my garden by tomorrow night, I'll put you out of teaching, you dopey drip!"

Mr McWeedie opened the door with a yoyo swinging from his finger.

Mr Spanker-Bacon shook his fist. "There's no mountain, you liar! Blimey, I'd give a million pounds to charity if I saw twenty tons of chocolate sitting outside my window."

"Done," said Mr McWeedie.

Next morning, after Ella had gone to school, a gleaming mound appeared in the garden. Her father hurried out to taste it. It was chocolate all right. "Strike me pink! What a sight!"

He rang the local paper to spread his amazing news and asked some nobs to Ella's birthday party. "It'll be Lord Spanker-Bacon soon," he boasted to Ella's mother. "Bacon and chocolate tycoon."

Now he'd got the chocolate, Mr Spanker-Bacon didn't want to pay one million pounds to charity. He wrote a cheque for *one pound* instead.

"That weedy wimp won't know," he chuckled as he posted it, "and I'll charge 'em all for eating my chocs as well." He bought a cash register on the way home and put up a sign. 'THIS WAY TO THE MYSTERY CHOCOLATE MOUNTAIN!'

Ella's party was a grand affair with the mayor and press. Her friends squealed with delight when they saw the mouth-watering chocolate mountain. But Tom couldn't believe his eyes. Why had Mr McWeedie given it to Ella Spanker-Bacon? Maybe he wasn't a wizard at all.

"I told you pinheads I'd be getting it, didn't I?" Ella boasted. "My dad paid a million pounds."

Games were played but the children could hardly wait for CHOCOLATE TIME.

"Me first!" Ella dug her spoon into the mountain and stuffed her mouth. "Ewghph . . .!"

The mayor choked on his hazlenut whirl and his false teeth flew out.

Mr Spanker-Bacon went purple.

"But it's pig poo!" said Tom.

"It's disgusting!" echoed the other guests. "How disgraceful."

In the commotion, only Tom saw Mr McWeedie pedalling away into the sky and laughing so much he nearly fell off his bike.

The Twenty Ton Chocolate Mountain

The day after the terrible birthday party disaster, Mr Spanker-Bacon drove round to see Mr McWeedie.

"I'm going to put you out of teaching, you loony lamp post. I gave a lot of money for that mountain of rubbish."

"You didn't, Spanker," said Mr McWeedie.

"Mr Spanker-Bacon jabbed a finger under his nose. "Are you calling me a liar?"

"Yes."

The next day Tom heard Mr Spanker-Bacon talking to the Head while Mr McWeedie was outside in the playground playing hopscotch.

"That McWeedie is a nutter and a crook. I want him out of this school."

"But Mr Spanker-Bacon," the Head pleaded, "the children love him."

Through the window Tom watched Mr McWeedie hopping. He shut his eyes. "Please don't let Ella's dad harm Weedy the Weed. Keep him away from our school."

Speeding home in a temper, Mr Spanker-Bacon crashed into a police car. He was so rude he was arrested and plonked in a police cell.

Tom wanted to warn Mr McWeedie about Ella's father but he never had the chance. He was still longing to go to the Chocolate Mountain but he couldn't talk about that in front of the others either. What he really needed was a friend to share his secrets.

"Don't tell anyone but Mr McWeedie is a wizard," Tom whispered to Marlon. "If you stare at him then shut your eyes and wish, the wish comes true."

"You never!" Marlon gasped, "Will he get me rollerblades and Gameboy and trainers?"

"Shut your eyes and see," Tom said. But when Marlon did it, nothing happened.

Tom nodded. "No, I suppose you're not the wizard type really."

"He's not a wizard, stupid," Marlon said. "I mean he'd have to live in a castle, wouldn'e, up the West End?"

They looked at Weedy slumped at his desk. His eyes were closed and his long thin legs spread out. One sock was red, the other blue. He always fell asleep after three helpings of syrup pudding for school dinner. He didn't look like a wizard.

"He *is* a wizard," Tom said crossly. "And so am I. I can prove it."

"Well, get somebody to punch that thieving kid Ella then. She nicked my fifty p."

While Tom closed his eyes, Daniel jumped up and pulled Ella's chair away so she sat on the floor.

Marlon laughed and laughed. "Brilliant!"

Ella shouted and pushed Daniel into Freddie, a fight started and the children grew noisy.

"Bet you can't magic a dinosaur, can you?" Marlon said.

Tom looked at Mr McWeedie who gave a faint snore. He wished . . . *hard*.

There was a rumbling, the school shook. A dark scaly shape filled the open window. A huge mouth opened and terrible teeth clattered.

"A monster . . . it's coming in! Ooo!" The children screamed and ran to hide.

"Crumbs!" muttered Tom.

"W..w..wicked!" Marlon stammered in a very small voice.

As the ancient beast opened its mouth and bellowed, Mr McWeedie woke up. "What the . . .? Oh go home, Gus," he said, quite crossly, and the creature vanished.

He stared hard at Tom. "You and I must have a talk."

Of course the children couldn't stop talking about the dinosaur at their window. Some were too frightened to go home.

Ella's father complained but the Head laughed. "Really Mr Spanker-Bacon! What will you say next? I expect poor McWeedie was only telling them a little story."

By the time the fuss died down, the term was nearly over. Mr McWeedie still hadn't said anything so Tom decided he'd better speak to him.

He cleaned his bicycle and waited. On the fourth night he spotted the wizard from his bedroom window. He pushed his bike onto the balcony, shut his eyes and took off.

The next minute he was away above the trees, rising higher and higher until he could no longer see his own block of flats.

"Mr McWeedie!" he shouted but he was lost. Suddenly, his bike swooped and began to fall. Faster and faster. WHOOOOSH!

He landed on his back in a soft bed of golden sunflowers. Around him was music from a chorus of tiny tinny voices.

"I hoped you'd come," said Mr McWeedie, picking up his bicycle. "There's a lot on tonight. The Yoyo Championship and the Dinosaurs' Race. We must hurry."

"Dinosaurs?" Tom said, alarmed. "Here?"

"Of course," Weedy replied. "They had to go somewhere when they died out. You'll ride Gus."

Tom stood up and froze with fright. Just ahead was a glade of trees. Dinosaurs were reaching up and tearing mouthfuls of spaghetti down.

Tom smiled politely: "I don't think I'll ride, thank you."

"Nonsense," replied Mr McWeedie. "Everybody does . . . if they want to get to the Chocolate Mountain. Gus is quite gentle. Look!"

Boys and girls were lining up while all the creatures were being saddled.

“Are girls wizards too?”

“They are these days,” said Weedy.

Gus seemed friendly as Tom was lifted onto his back. Strands of spaghetti still hung from his mouth.

“Hold tight!” called Mr McWeedie. “See you at the Chocolate Mountain! Winner gets first bite!”

He rode ahead on his bike trailing a clump of spaghetti. The animals thundered after him, bellowing.

“Come on, Gus!” shouted Tom.

Tom didn't even know he and Gus won that race. He forgot everything when he saw the Twenty Ton Chocolate Mountain. He led Gus towards it in a daze. It was a magical sight!

The Chocolate Mountain rose from a platform of marzipan. Planks of peppermint cream were laid across it. The next layer was fudge. Up and up it went into the starlit sky, gleaming pink here, vanilla there. To reach it you walked through lines of butterscotch candles. On the grass were little baskets of jelly wizards.

Tom couldn't say a word.

"Tom is the winner," Mr McWeedie declared, as the other children clustered round with their puffing dinosaurs. "His prize is first taste of the Twenty Ton Chocolate Mountain. He will then become a wizard."

Tom's mouth was watering. He reached for the spoon and dug it into a turret of strawberry cream.

"Do you want to be a wizard?" demanded Weedy. "Think hard."

Tom put out his tongue to lick the chocolate. He'd nearly touched it when he had a thought. "Will I be able to go home?"

"Well, not really," Weedy said, "not when you're a wizard."

The chocolate was so tempting. It couldn't matter just eating a bit. He raised his spoon again. He *had* to taste it now.

But he thought of his parents and his hamster and never seeing them again. He shut his mouth just in time. Some chocolate spilt on his pyjamas.

Tom started to feel giddy. Something was tugging him away into the air. He was going . . . he couldn't stop himself. Mr McWeedie waved and Gus bellowed.

He woke up in his own bed and guessed he'd had a dream. He lay there thinking about it.

"You're not to eat chocolate in bed," his mother said, when she came in and pulled back the duvet. "This strawberry stuff is all over your pyjamas. Who gave it to you?"

"Mr McWeedie," Tom answered. "It's from the Twenty Ton Chocolate Mountain. I'll ask old Weedy more about it next term."

But when he went back to school, the wizard wasn't there.

Look out for more magical books in the Storybooks series:

Magic Mark by Helen Muir

George wants to be a magician when he grows up. But when he tries out his spells, they always end in disaster . . .

A Magic Birthday by Adèle Geras

Maddy is looking forward to her birthday party, but there is just one thing missing and Maddy is very worried . . .

Wonderwitch by Helen Muir

Wonderwitch was tired of all her old spells, so she decided to try something quite different!

Princess by Mistake by Penelope Lively

What would *you* do if, one ordinary Wednesday afternoon, your sister was suddenly kidnapped by a knight in full armour riding an enormous black horse?

The Magic of the Mummy by Terry Deary

In the Museum of Mystery, Cleo is promised a thousand pounds if she can decipher the Mummy's secret message . . .

TV Genie by John Talbot

The old TV set Paul discovered in his grandfather's attic was no ordinary set – it had black-and-white magic!